A Tricky I

Diane Simmons

abuddhapress@yahoo.com

i

ISBN: 9798868242526

To Geeta
I hope you enjoy it!
Diane Simmons x

The following is a work of fiction. Any similarities to actual people, places, or events, unless deliberately expressed otherwise by the author are purely coincidental.

For my family, with love

Contents:

The Spare Seat

At break, Jennifer and her gang hang around the new girl. Lorna's pretty with neat clothes, so the boys hover too, gawping. Boys don't gawp at me. My straggly hair's not blonde like hers and my home-made dress has patches on the elbows.

Girls clamber straight away to lend Lorna their felt pens, to show her the way to the toilets, to offer her sweeties. By mid-week, she's lost none of her appeal. It appears she's clever. In maths, she's moved to the spare seat on the top table with Jennifer and all the other brainy ones. I'm dead mad – I've had my eye on that seat since last week when one of the boys was moved down to our table for swearing.

Still fuming at home time, I'm rummaging in my school bag, when I hear a throat clear and look up. Jennifer and Lorna are standing in front of me, sniggering.

'Is that right you're English?' Lorna asks.

'I've lived here since I was two!'

She snorts. 'Jesus, you sound like the bloody Queen!'

That evening, when I've washed the dishes for my mum, I go off to the swing park to see if there's anyone about. It's empty except for a dog and the town's tramp. Freezing, I head to the swings to try to warm myself up. I'm just getting going when I see Lorna and Jennifer. They're marching towards me. Soon, they're right there, staring. I slow the swing down with my toes. 'What're you looking at?' I ask.

'I'm no' sure – the label's come off,' Lorna says.

'Ha bloody ha,' I say. 'You're awfy full of yourself for a new girl.'

'What do you ken, Elspeth? You're no' even from round here.'

'Neither are you,' I laugh. 'You're from Glasgow. Glasgow! Everyone knows it's a dump.'

I am on the ground. Lorna's pulled me off the swing and soon we're wrestling and thrashing our arms and legs about. Just as I'm flagging, Lorna stands up and shouts,

'She hit ma eye, she hit ma eye!'

I get up and stare her in the face. Her left eye's already beginning to swell and she's crying like a baby.

I brush myself down. 'Just mind who you mess wi,' I say in my best Scottish accent.

At break the next morning, a crowd gathers round me desperate to hear how I hammered the new girl. For the rest of the morning, they're all over me. I don't let on that it was an accident, that my foot must have slipped and kicked her eye.

Later that afternoon, after the results of an algebra test, our maths teacher decides that Lorna's not quite as brilliant as it first appeared. She's on a warning to improve or risk moving down a table.

I tidy my desk in anticipation.

Things in Common

I'm sitting on my garden wall, bored out of my skull, when I see the new girl from school. I nearly leg it back inside. I've not been near her since I gave her that black eye.

'Is that your house, Elspeth?' Lorna says. 'I stay in thae flats round the corner.'

I nod, surprised. I had Lorna down as living in one of the private houses on the other side of town, not on our council scheme.

'Your jeans are fab,' she says.

I glance down at my hems. They look great since I embroidered them with the names of all The Bay City Rollers. It took me yonks. 'Thanks. Alan's my favourite,' I lie. I never let on to anyone that I like Les best – I've no chance of getting *him*.

'I've got all their records,' she says. 'Do you want to come over to mine and play them? Ma mum's at work.'

I look from left to right, then back again. Her pals must be somewhere, waiting to pounce.

'It's okay,' she says, laughing. 'I'll no' bash you!'

4

I decide to risk it and follow her to the flats. The lift's broken and we race up the three flights of stairs. I win and she looks impressed.

When we get inside, her flat's really messy with boxes everywhere. There's orange swirly wallpaper half ripped off the walls.

'Ma mum's gonnae unpack soon,' she says. 'She's taken on extra shifts at work.'

She doesn't mention her dad. Maybe she's not got one. It'd be great to not be the only one in our class without a dad.

We have a drink of juice and two jammy dodgers each, then she takes me through to her room to show me her Rollers records. She's got millions.

'Jennifer makes fun of me for still liking The Rollers,' I say. 'She says they're rubbish.'

'Jennifer's awfy mean to you sometimes.'

I shrug. 'Not always. We used to be best pals in primary school, but I'm not like her and all the others – they're clever.'

'You did well in that geography test yesterday,' she says. 'You got the same as me.'

Lorna laughs when she realises what she's said. She's got a nice laugh.

'Sorry. You ken what I mean,' she says. 'Dinnae put yourself down.'

'It's not just the clever thing,' I say. 'They all do ballet and tap and go to Spain for their holidays. And they've got brilliant clothes. Me and my mum don't have the money for things like that. And me being English doesn't help either when they're looking for reasons...'

'I'm sorry I made fun of you for being English the other day,' she says. 'I shouldnae have started that fight.'

'S'okay. I'm sorry about bashing your eye.'

'Which part of England are you from, Elspeth?'

'London. My mum's from Elgin and I pretended to everyone I was born there too, but they all found out I was lying.'

She laughs again. 'I'm from London too. But I telt them I was born in Glasgow.'

When I've taken in what she said, I giggle. Soon, we're both helpless, collapsed on the floor. We're still laughing, when I check the clock. 'Aw heck, it's time for my paper round!' I say. 'I'd best go. Thanks for asking me round to yours – it's been great!'

She's about to say something, but I get in first. 'I won't tell,' I say. 'About the London thing.' I grin at her. 'Pals don't tell.'

6

Odette

'Could I not just try a ballet tester lesson, Mum? Everyone else goes. They get to put on a concert and everything.'

She doesn't even look up from her ironing. 'I've said before, Elspeth – you wouldn't like it.'

At school the next week, Lorna hands me a ticket. 'Madame gave me some free ones.'

I don't believe her, but I put it into my pencil case, grin all the way through French.

I'm still grinning at home-time as I run to the paper shop. I do my round in record time, rush home and bolt dinner. As soon as I've done the dishes, I leg it to the church hall and manage to get a seat right at the front.

It's the older girls on first and my stomach does a flip when the music starts. They all look so bonnie in their white tutus and feather headdresses. Dance of the Swans is my favourite. I can't believe how good they are and clap till my hands are sore. Next, everyone I know comes on and they all do ballet exercises like they're in their Saturday morning class. The old biddy beside me mutters that the exercises are boring and I give her a look. How can she think that?

I concentrate, try to take everything in.

When I get home, my mum is on the settee under a blanket watching a Morecambe and Wise repeat. I go upstairs, get out my *Princess Ballet Annual* and look through the photos again: Moira Shearer in *Red Shoes*, Alicia Markova in *Giselle*, Rudolf Nureyev in *Coppelia*. They're all brilliant, but it's the one of Margot Fonteyn as Odette that makes me ache.

Shivering, I undress, put on my black swim suit and party slipperettes and tie up my hair in a bun. In front of the long mirror, I practise the five positions, go through the exercises I saw the others do earlier. I study the Margot Fonteyn picture again, try to copy her arabesque. But I'm rubbish. I've not got a clue.

Almost crying, I tip out the money from my piggy bank onto the bed, calculate what I'll need for Guides, for the school trip to Edinburgh Castle, for my mum's birthday next week. Maybe if I stopped Guides, sold my uniform, scrounged a few quid off Mum...

And then I remember the hole in my school shoes, remember Mum's face when I told her.

Sighing, I get changed, kick the swim suit under the bed then go downstairs and make Mum some cocoa with the last of the milk.

'How was the concert?' she asks when I take it in to her.

I remember what the old biddy said and just lie. 'It was a wee bit boring.'

I sit down with her and watch the end of the show. The lady who reads the news is on with Eric and Ernie. She's dancing – kicking her legs up really high. She's amazing. I bet *she* had lessons – ballet, tap, the lot. Sticking my tongue out at her, I get up and switch off the telly, pull the blanket round me and cuddle up to my mum for warmth.

Dance of the Cuckoos

Lorna's mum borrowed a bowler hat for her from a pal. But my mum doesn't know folk like that. Mum said not to worry and made me one out of a Corn Flakes packet. It looks stupid. I never wanted to go as Laurel and Hardy for Halloween anyway. And I don't get why I have to be the fat one. But I always seem to give in to Lorna. I'm pleased though that she isn't hanging around with that Thomas Ferguson tonight rather than coming guising with me. Thomas Ferguson thinks guising's childish, but it'll be me and Lorna who have the money for fireworks, not him.

Lorna calls for me at six and teaches me the Laurel and Hardy dance she's seen on the telly – something about cuckoos. We practise in my lounge until we're sore laughing and my mum gets fed up and shoos us out the door. Lorna's not got round to making a turnip lantern, so I give her mine.

The first neighbour we try is Mrs Grant at number five. 'It's fearfully cold, girls,' she says when she answers the door. 'Come away in and do your turn.'

We go through to her lounge and Lorna starts humming the Laurel and Hardy tune again. Trying to keep together, we kick our legs out to the side, put on daft faces. Mrs Grant claps her hands hard when we've finished and hands us 50p each and some gob stoppers.

Feeling happy with our haul, we go to the next five houses in my street. Everyone gives us money except the rich old biddy on the corner. All we get from her is a bag of monkey nuts. We're walking away, moaning, when I hear a shout.

'Over here, Lorna!'

It's Thomas Ferguson.

Thomas is standing under the lamp post looking gorgeous in his new leather jacket. Lorna grins like a mad thing when she sees him, almost chucks her lantern and bowler at me and rushes over. They're soon snogging. I look away, pick at my chipped nail varnish until she shouts over, 'That's me done guising, Elspeth. See you tomorrow.'

I wave a cheery goodbye like I'm not bothered. As I walk away down the street, I chuck my hat into the mean old biddy's hedge and put on Lorna's proper bowler instead. It fits fine and I start humming the theme tune again. But I don't dance.

It's a dance meant for two.

Blood

Jennifer and Lorna are leaning on the wall outside the science block, poring over this week's *Jackie*. They're all pally again and are forever giggling about boys they fancy or what group they like. Lorna pretends to Jennifer that she's a fan of The Stranglers, but I know for a fact she's still mad on The Rollers.

I walk up to them, try to act casual. 'My mum's had the tops of her toes cut off,' I say.

Jennifer looks up, sneers. 'Aye, right.'

I give her a wee stare. 'She has! They chopped the top bits off, cut out the middle, then put the tops back on. That's why I had school dinners last week!'

'Prove it,' Lorna says.

In the morning, Jennifer and Lorna are waiting for me by the school gates. 'Have you got your mum's toes in that bag?' Jennifer asks and they both giggle.

I reach into my school bag and they step back. I pull out two long needles. 'The doctors put these through my mum's toes when they took the tops off,' I say. 'To stop them collapsing.'

Jennifer walks back towards me and peers at them, but Lorna screams and legs it into the playground.

'What's wrong wi' you?' Jennifer shouts over to her. 'There's no' even any blood on them!'

I think about making fun of Lorna too, but I don't quite dare. Instead, I look at Jennifer and raise my eyebrows.

She grins at me. 'What a baby!'

I try not to, but I'm soon telling Jennifer everything I can remember about my mum's operation and she listens engrossed. 'There *was* loads of blood on the needles,' I say. 'And the corks the doctors put on the ends of them were covered in it!'

'Have you got the corks? Are they in your bag? Can I see?' she asks.

'My mum keeps them on the mantlepiece. Come round on Saturday and I'll show you if you want.'

She puts her head on one side. 'I might.'

The bell rings for school to start and I follow her in, trying not to smile. Maybe she'll come round, maybe she'll not. But at least she's thinking about it. Thinking about me.

The Gay Gordons

All the girls in my class are in a huddle in the playground, plotting. As soon as the teacher announced the date of our Christmas party, I knew they'd start.

There's no point in me joining the plotters. I'll not get a say. Jennifer and her pals always decide everyone's dancing partners. For weeks before the party they're off giggling, passing round notes, bagsying the gorgeous boys for themselves. Last year I got stuck with Rory McMaster. We got in a right tangle doing The Gay Gordons. Rory's not bad looking, but he's really pale and his spikey hair makes him look like Oor Wullie.

I head off to the football field. Ewan Wilson has the ball. He always has the ball. And he's always Jennifer's dancing partner. But me and Ewan hang out some nights and play football – I bet he'd rather dance with me.

I run my fingers through my hair, try to untangle the worst of the knots and march over towards Ewan. It's not until I'm near him that my legs begin to wobble. But he smiles and kicks the ball towards me.

'Fancy a game, Elspeth?' he asks.

I shake my head. 'No, you're fine – I've a skirt on.'

He snorts and I look down at my skirt – it's all creased and covered in grass stains.

'Aye, I can see you wouldnae be wanting to spoil it!' he says as he walks away shaking his head and laughing. I feel like that messy monkey I saw on the school trip to Edinburgh Zoo – the one with its fur covered in squashed fruit.

I want to bolt, but I walk away slowly, try not to notice him scoring another of his perfect goals. Near the playground, I see Rory McMaster coming towards me. He's acting really weird – taking funny wee steps, his arms all over the place. When he starts walking backwards, then twists round, I see that he's dancing. He waves at me and runs over.

'Would you care to dance, Modom?' he asks.

He sounds stupid, but I let him take my hand.

When we've got our limbs sorted, he starts to hum the tune to the Gay Gordons and leads me through the dance. He's magnificent, in control. We get through the tricky bit no bother and he twirls me round and round like he's been practising for weeks.

When we stop and he bows, then gives me a shy wee smile, I realise he has.

16

Saturday Nights

Not wanting a repeat of the piss-taking I got for liking Wings, I almost don't mention it at school. 'Did you see that ice skating programme about John Curry winning the gold?' I ask Jennifer eventually.

'Aye, it was brill!' she says. 'They have a DJ at the rink, Saturdays. We should go.'

I quickly add up in my head how much birthday money I've got left, then nod. Jennifer pokes Lorna in the arm to get her attention. 'Do ya fancy it?' she asks.

We're not at the ice rink half an hour before Lorna's off up the back seats snogging some boy with dirty finger nails. I glare at any other boys who look like they might approach and Jennifer and I have a laugh trying to stay upright, clinging on to each other for support.

I'm soon much better than Jennifer. I love it. I don't even mind the cramp in my toes or the manky café that smells of stale fat. And I manage to get round the rink on my own, even get to the centre where all the posers are hanging out doing spins and jumps. I don't abandon

Jennifer for long though. I take her hand and help her round the rink, will her to enjoy it as much as me.

Lorna goes off to a party with some boy the next week, but I don't miss her. It's great having Jennifer all to myself at the rink. It feels like when we were wee and used to hang out together all the time. Desperate to keep her amused, I tell her daft jokes and she laughs, but spends most of the evening ogling some guy with David Cassidy hair.

'Will you chase after him for me?' she asks. 'I'd never catch him.'

It takes me four goes round the ice and two falls before I crash into the barrier next to him.

'You need to learn how to stop, hen,' he says, and winks at me. 'I can show you, if you want.'

'Will you go out with my pal?'

He laughs. 'Which one's she?'

'Over there – the pretty one with the blue jumper.'

'Perhaps? Send her over.'

I skate slowly. I can feel him staring and I'm desperate not to land on my bum. I bite my lip, give Jennifer a wee shrug. 'Sorry, he's already got a girlfriend.'

At registration on the Monday, Jennifer looks up from her jotter. 'Me and Lorna are going to Jamie Ross's party next Saturday, so we'll no' be going skating.'

I stare at my book, try not to show I'm upset. I loved hanging round with Jennifer again, loved pretending she's still my best pal and I'd loved it at the rink too.

I look around the classroom for someone else I could ask to go with me. But there's no one else. There's never really been anyone else.

Dancing

Rory McMaster corners me after double geography.

'You ken how we had a go at the Gay Gordons the other day?'

'Aye, you were great.'

He does one of his wee bows. 'I've been learning Scottish Country Dancing at the church hall every Thursday. We do Highland Dancing too. Do you want to come along?'

I hesitate and he goes bright red.

'No' like that,' he says. 'I mean I'm no' asking you out or anything…'

I smile, tell him I know what he meant, but I don't answer his question. I'm fed up of having to make excuses for not doing things. And this is dancing. I bloody love dancing. I sigh. 'How much is it?'

'It's only 75p a week,' he says.

I can't imagine thinking 75p was nothing. I get £3 for doing my paper round and I've to pay for everything out of that. Maybe if I took on a Sunday paper round too? 'What do the girls wear?' I ask.

'Your gutties and a skirt would do.'

I picture myself turning up in my gym shoes and school skirt, imagine the looks. 'I don't think I can.'

When I get to school the next day, there's a plastic bag on top of my locker. Expecting something gross, I peer inside – it's a pair of dancing pumps.

I hound Rory down at break. 'I can't take these,' I say. 'They must've cost a bomb.'

'They were my sister's,' he says. 'They don't fit her anymore.'

I examine the pumps again. There's no sign of any wear – there's not a single mark on them. He must think I'm daft.

'That's nice of your sister,' I say. I stare at the pumps, then at Rory's worried face and grin at him. 'See you there on Thursday,' I say.

'Seven o'clock,' he says, and grins back.

Cabbage Pie

Mum passes me a butter bean rissole. It's really grey-looking.

'Are you sure you wouldn't rather have a meat pie?' she asks.

I shake my head and bite into the rissole. It's all claggy and I heave. I don't let on it's horrible though. Instead, I suck all the gunge off my teeth, force it down and smile at her. 'Is this out of that George Bernard Shaw vegetarian cookbook you got from the library?' I ask.

She giggles. 'Yes. He was a funny wee soul. He wouldn't let his housekeeper cash cheques at the butcher's.'

I'd not a clue being a vegetarian would be so hard, that there would be so many rules. Jennifer said that not eating meat was a doddle and showed us pictures of pigs in tiny pens. But her mum makes food for her from peppers and other posh things she buys in Marks and Spencer's. That's not going to happen in *my* house – most of our food's out of dented tins from the Co-op.

At lunchtime, the day after the rissole, I look across at Jennifer chatting with her pals and wonder if she'll come over. She'd looked really pleased when I told her I wanted to become a vegetarian, had let me hang out with her at break for weeks. And she always wanted to know what I'd got in my packed lunch, would quiz me about what I'd eaten for dinner. But last week when she found out that Mum had made me a cabbage pie, she laughed for ages. She's not bothered asking since.

The next Saturday morning, first thing, I take *The George Bernard Shaw Vegetarian Cookbook* back to the library and renew it like my mum asked me to. I'm fine with her still using it – she can manage the recipes and nearly all the ingredients are cheap enough. I scour the shelves though for a better cookbook, search for one with colourful pictures of food I'd love to try, dishes that I can learn the names of, ones that I can practise describing so well it sounds as if I eat them every day.

Support

I sit down on the wall and take a *Vogue* out of my bag. I'm shattered. Mine's a rubbish paper round. The folk round this way all live in houses the size of castles with drives a mile long. The round takes ages. It's not like doing terraces or flats. Even in the housing scheme I go to next, everyone's got huge front gardens.

I stare at the cover of the magazine. Farah Fawcett was on the front a while back, but I don't recognise the woman on this one. She's really skinny and you can see all the bones in her chest – she's got no knockers at all. Not like me. Mine are ginormous. When I do the Highland Fling at dancing class, they bounce up and down and all the boys snigger and call me names on the way home. My dancing teacher said I needed a better bra and showed me a Playtex Cross Your Heart one in her Freemans catalogue. It costs a bomb, so I've taken on an extra round.

It's not all bad. I love reading the comics and magazines. I like the problem pages in *Cosmopolitan* best. I was going to write in but everything in there's about sex, so I did one to Cathy and Claire in *Jackie* instead. I didn't send it though. Everyone at school would have known it was me.

When I get home, Mum's already got dinner ready. It's macaroni cheese pie. I love macaroni cheese pie. We used to have it all the time when I was wee.

      'This is brilliant!' I say, as I eat a bit. 'Is it from the baker's?'

      'Cheeky monkey. I made it myself.'

      I look up at Mum and grin. She's been going mad cooking all the time – not just special vegetarian stuff for me, but cakes and fruit pies too. She even made shortbread last week when she found some cheap butter in the Co-op. The meals have been great, but she shouldn't be doing so much. 'All that standing in the kitchen can't be good for your feet,' I say. 'You know what the doctor said after your operation.'

      'Och, don't worry, Elspeth,' she says. 'I'm fine.'

      It's easy for her to say not to worry, but what if she gets worse, if her arthritis moves to another part of her body? I can't stand watching her in pain.

      'Talking of worrying,' she says. 'I found that letter you wrote to *Jackie*.' She presses her lips together. 'I wasn't noseying – I was just

25

after borrowing that Jane Austen book you're reading at school and the letter was inside.'

I stop eating, stare at my plate. I can't even look at her. What did I write? I know I told them about her crying, about the pain. Did I say about being fed up of all the chores I have to do, about us always being skint?

When I eventually look up, she just smiles. 'I bumped into that nice dancing teacher of yours,' she says. 'Her husband works at the brewery – he's been looking for someone for the office. I've to start on Monday.'

I can't speak at first. A job? She's not worked for years. I'm about to object when she pats my hand.

'I'll be sitting down most of the time,' she says. 'I'm sure I'll cope. And we'll be better off now so you can stop that extra paper round. You've enough on.'

She gets up from the table and passes me a plastic bag. 'I ordered you this,' she says.

I open the bag, look at her and grin. It's a bra. A Playtex bra!

'See if it fits,' she says. 'Mrs Abbot can send it back if it doesn't.'

I rush upstairs to try it on. When I go back into the kitchen, I jump about, dance a wee dance. Mum laughs and claps her hands.

'Perfect,' she says. 'Your bosoms hardly moved at all!'

I giggle at the word 'bosoms'. Carry on giggling till I can't stop.

At it Again

Our French teacher's at it again. I don't know how Jimmy Anderson
copes. Today, Jimmy gets 15 per cent in the test and Mr Johnstone swats
him over the head, then slams the test paper down on Jimmy's desk. No
doubt it'll be Margo or one of the others who dodge off school who'll be
for it next.

I'm just praying for 50 per cent.

My hands get sweaty as Mr Johnstone thrashes about the
classroom chucking test papers back, making horrible remarks as he
goes. I revised loads, but that doesn't mean anything – there was still
tons of things I wasn't sure about. It's just not fair – some folk in our
class, like Jennifer, never have to pore over books for hours – they just
seem to know things.

When Mr Johnstone gets to those who've passed, he calms
down and I even hear the odd 'Not bad' or 'That's better'. By the time
he gets to those who've got 65 per cent, he's almost smiling.

Soon, there's only a few of us left.

I look across at Jennifer. She's doodling on her jotter, but she sees me and mouths to ask what I got. I shrug and her gob drops open. She leans over and whispers,

'He must have lost yours.'

I nod. Of course. Why else would I not have had mine back? Or maybe he's not lost it, but he's saving it till the end so he can call me out to the front of the class and make fun of me, like he did with Patsy last week when she'd been off with the flu. He loves making folk look like idiots. And he loves giving us the belt. I've not been whacked since primary three but I can still remember how much it stung. I start to cry, but quickly wipe my eyes. He mustn't see I'm frightened.

Seconds later, he's by Rory's desk. Rory's one of his favourites and Mr Johnstone gives him a 'Well done' and pats him on the shoulder.

I look around the classroom. There's just me and Jennifer left. Me and Jennifer! Mr Johnstone hesitates, then frowning, he comes towards me. I see a big fat 87 per cent circled in red on my test paper.

'It's not like you to get such a good mark, Elspeth,' he says. 'I hope there was no cheating going on. Perhaps you should see me after class.'

I hear sniggering from everywhere, see Jennifer out of the corner of my eye. She's laughing really loudly, nudging the girl next to her. I want to punch her. I want to punch everyone.

Rory puts his hand up and shouts out, 'Elspeth worked really hard for the test, sir – she's brilliant at verbs – she helped me with my homework last week when I got stuck!'

Mr Johnstone studies his face, sniffs.

I can't breathe.

'Is that right, Rory?' he asks. Rory nods and Mr Johnstone turns to face me. 'In that case, well done, Elspeth, well done! Keep it up.'

I look over at Jennifer. She's stopped laughing and her gob's hanging open again. She looks stupid.

I smile at her, then at Mr Johnstone. 'I'll do my best.'

A Nasty Taste

I'm on the way to Rory's for dinner before dancing, when I see Jennifer and Lorna coming out of the chippie. They're both carrying pokes of chips and meat pies, stuffing their faces as if they're starving.

I can't believe Jennifer's eating meat after all she said. She knows fine well I only became a vegetarian because of her.

By the time I get to Rory's house, I'm crying. I wait outside to give myself a minute, but his mum sees me through the glass and opens the door.

'Come away in, hen,' she says. She studies my face. 'Are you okay?'

'I'm fine, Mrs McMaster. It's just the wind making my eyes water.'

Rory comes downstairs and we go through to watch *Blue Peter* on his big colour telly. I tell him about Jennifer and the pie and he tuts. He always tuts when I talk about Jennifer.

He nods at the telly. 'We should go on there. They'd lap up Highland Dancing on *Blue Peter* – we could have a piper on with us. It'd be great!'

31

I laugh. We're good at dancing, but we're not that good.

Rory's mum calls us to the table. She looks a bit worried when she hands me my plate. 'That vegetarian sausage mix doesn't look very appetising, Elspeth,' she says. 'I've made it into sausage shapes for you, but...'

'They look smashing, Mrs McMaster.'

I cut off a bit and eat it. It's all gritty so I dip it in ketchup but it doesn't help. I think about Jennifer and the meat pie and get mad again. I'd kill for some meat right now.

His mum hovers for a minute, then goes back to the kitchen. Rory stares at my dinner and pulls a face. 'Those sausages look horrible,' he says.

'They are a bit. But don't tell your mum. It's kind of her to make me special food every week.'

'She likes having you around,' he says. Grinning, he stabs my sausages with his fork, wraps them in his hanky and hides them in his pocket. Winking, he passes me one of his proper ones.

I giggle and bite into the crispy skin. It's brilliant. He's a pal, Rory – a real pal.

Hand in Hand

'I cannae do it,' Rory says.

I stop fiddling with my socks and stare at him. He looks awful – even more peely-wally than normal. I tut. 'Don't be daft – you'll be great!'

'I mean it – some folk in here will have been dancing since they were wee.' He nods towards a group in the corner of the room. 'They're from that posh school my cousin Alastair goes to. They've loads of brilliant dance teachers – we cannae compete with them.'

I know the boys he's talking about – they look smart in their waistcoats and matching kilts. They're even wearing berets. Mind, I look brilliant too in the red kilt and white blouse our teacher lent me and Rory's mum went all the way to Glasgow to buy his outfit. He's not looking his best today though.

'We'll be fine,' I say, straightening his bowtie.

'I should've gone in for the Highland Fling,' he says, flopping down on a chair. 'I'm rubbish at the Sword Dance – I'm no' doing it,' he says and heaves.

I look around for our dance teacher, but I can't see her. I've not got a clue what to do. I'm not dancing if Rory isn't. Swearing, I rummage in my rucksack, find an old plastic bag and chuck it at him. 'Use that if you're gonna be ill,' I say.

Rory's still clutching the bag five minutes later when an older boy walks over. The boy's gorgeous with dark curly hair, but he's got the kind of face that makes me want to belt him one.

'You've not grown out of throwing up then?' he asks Rory. He turns and grins at me. 'My dear cousin was always being sick when he was little – or wetting the bed!' He ruffles Rory's hair. 'You just need more practice – our school enters us into competitions all the time – we usually win. But then we're not taught by some old wifie in a church hall.'

I jut out my chin. 'Our teacher says nerves are good, that they make you perform better.' I smile at Rory. 'Isn't that right?'

'Aye. And she kens what she's on about. Mrs Abbot's won tons of prizes *and* she's danced all over the world – she's even done a Highland Fling for the Pope.'

Alastair snorts. 'The Pope?'

34

'Aye,' says Rory, getting out of his chair and puffing out his chest. 'The Pope! He was very appreciative – he's a big fan of Highland dancing!'

I nod. 'He likes to watch it on the telly.'

Gob open, Alastair stares at me, then at Rory. I look up at the clock. 'Time's getting on, you'd best be away.'

He leaves and Rory starts to giggle. Soon, we're both bent double laughing. When we eventually recover, I reach for his hand. 'Ready to go?'

He smooths down his kilt, adjusts his sporran, then takes my hand in his. 'Aye, I'm ready to go.'

Launch Pad

Our guidance teacher sounds bored by the time she gets to me. 'So, Elspeth, what do *you* want to do when you leave school?'

I mumble, 'Nurse.' I'm the fifth girl to say that, so no one laughs, or throws their rubbers at me like they did earlier when Rory announced he wanted to be an astronaut.

'We don't have rockets in Scotland, stupit!' Jennifer sneered at him when he gave his answer. 'We're no' American!'

Mrs Kelly told Jennifer to be quiet, but I could tell she agreed with her.

I'm with Rory on the astronaut thing. Not that I want to go into space, but I like to dream about things too. Like how one day I might get to be top of the class, or get to dance on the telly. Just last week me and Rory won prizes for our dancing and we've not been learning long, so maybe the top of the class thing's possible too – children develop at different ages. I've got Pythagoras sorted now and yesterday I didn't have a clue.

My mum's got no patience with me. 'There's nothing wrong with being ordinary,' she says. 'Being clever or famous isn't the be-all.'

I'd like the chance to find out.

The teacher perks up when it's Jennifer's turn. 'And how about you?' she asks.

'I'm no' sure,' Jennifer says and gives one of her sickly smiles. 'I like babies.'

Mrs Kelly gives her a huge smile. 'Working with children can certainly be rewarding. Perhaps you should be thinking about becoming a children's doctor or a surgeon.'

Jennifer shrugs. 'I'm no' fussed about a job. I'd like to stay home like ma mum.'

Mrs Kelly looks like she's been slapped. Until a few weeks ago, Jennifer was top of the class in everything, was forever bragging about how clever she was, how she was going to be a doctor or lawyer when she grew up. Now all she seems bothered about is snogging boys.

If I get to be top of the class, then maybe *I* could be a doctor. I'd be a kind one like the doctor who looks after my mum. And me and Rory could go and visit all the old biddies in nursing homes, do a wee dance for them to cheer them up. Old biddies love dancing.

When the teacher's busy quizzing everyone else, I sneak a peek at Rory. He's drawing a rocket, pressing hard down on his jotter when he adds the clouds of smoke.

It's preparing to launch. Just like me and Rory.

Previously Published

Grateful acknowledgment is made to the following journals where these stories first appeared in an earlier form:

'The Spare Seat' (as 'Top Table'), Frome Festival website, 2011

'Odette', National Flash Fiction Day Anthology *And We Pass Through*, 2019

'Dance of the Cuckoos', *Splonk*, 2020

'Blood' (as 'A Delicate Operation'), *Hysteria 3*, 2014

'The Gay Gordons' (as 'Dancing Partners'), National Flash Fiction Day Anthology *Sleep is a Beautiful Colour*, 2017

'Saturday Nights', Retreat West Anthology *What was Left*, 2017

'Dancing', Bath Flash Fiction Anthology *Restore to Factory Settings*, 2020

'Cabbage Pie', Reflex Fiction website, 2022

'Support', National Flash Fiction Day Anthology *Legerdemain*, 2021

'Launch Pad', National Flash Fiction Day Anthology *Eating My Words*, 2014

Acknowledgements

My first thanks must go to my husband Phil for being a constant source of encouragement and patience, particularly with tech problems. I'd also like to thank my children and their partners for their love and support. Special thanks must also go to Ally Laver and Jeanette Sheppard for their help with the cover of the book – their input was invaluable. Next, I would like to thank Jude Higgins who relentlessly (in a good way) encourages me to submit and to believe in what I've written. I would also very much like to thank Damhnait Monaghan and Jude Higgins for their generous quotes for the back of the book; Karen Jones and Jenny Woodhouse for their rigorous proofreading; Patsy McClay and Karen Jones for checking Scottish dialect and Alison Woodhouse for so often being a listening ear. Thanks also to Red at Alien Buddha for all his hard work. Finally, I'd like to thank everyone who has ever supported me in any way, particularly the flash community for their input and all the fun.

About the Author

Diane Simmons lives in Bath, UK. She is a co-director of National Flash Fiction Day, UK and a former director of Flash Fiction Festivals, UK. She has been widely published in magazines such as *New Flash Fiction Review*, *Mslexia*, *Splonk* and *FlashBack Fiction* and placed in numerous writing competitions. 'Finding a Way', her flash collection on the theme of grief, was published by Ad Hoc Fiction in 2019 and shortlisted in the Saboteur Awards in the Best Short Story Collection category. Her historical novella-in-flash 'An Inheritance' was published by V. Press in 2020 and shortlisted in the Saboteur Awards Best Novella category. A former reader for the international Bath Short Story Award, she has been a judge for several flash competitions including Flash 500, New Zealand's Micro Madness, NFFD Micro Fiction Competition, and many online Flash Fiction Festival competitions. She is an editor for FlashFlood and has co-edited six flash fiction festival anthologies. You can read more about Diane on her website www.dianesimmons.co.uk and connect with her on X @scooterwriter and Bluesky @scooterwriter.bsky.social

Printed in Great Britain
by Amazon